All inquiries should be addressed to:

STERLING DESIGN INC & PUBLISHING

PO BOX 52

DULUTH MN 55801-0052

© 1991 Richard Mosse

© 1991 Bun-Bun's Brook Trout

Illustrations: by © Richard Mosse

Editor: Jeff S. Sonstegard

STERLING DESIGN INC & PUBLISHING

ISBN 0-9630328-1-X

Library of Congress Catalog Card Number: 91-067654

2 3 4 5 6 7 8 9 10

Printed in Korea

Bun-Bun's Brook Trout

by

Richard Mosse

for Lura & David

Bun-Bun was daydreaming as he lay in the grass by his house. He looked
down with one eye at little bugs in the grass. Then he looked up
with the other eye at the sky.

In the sky clouds drifted like trout in a stream. And in the grass the bugs
swayed on the stems, as if they were attached to small green fly rods.

"It must be a sign ... A sign that I should go fishing," mused Bun-Bun.

It took very little to inspire Bun-Bun for an afternoon of trout fishing.

Bun-Bun jumped up, and ran into his house to put on his fishing outfit. He
pulled on his hip boots, slung his net and creel over his shoulder,
and then grabbed his fly rod and lucky fishing hat.

All set for the stream, Bun-Bun rambled across the field behind his house
and into the woods.

As he walked, he hummed a quiet tune,
"Hmm trout, hum trouts, big trout hmm."

Bun-Bun soon came to a meandering little stream in the depths of the big woods. He sat for a spell on a mossy old rock, where he set up his rod, and watched the stream slither around a bend.

Beyond the bend, the stream slid quietly into Bun-Bun's favorite big pool.
He crept silently through the brush, so as not to scare the trout away.
Carefully he pushed aside one last branch and there it was....

The deep dark pool, with the mossy log with a fern on top!
It was the pool of his dreams, and the home of huge wild brook trout. The
pool had been unknown to man or rabbit before Bun-Bun found it.
Since then it had become Bun-Bun's secret spot.

Bun-Bun trembled with joy as he thought of the big trout swimming
beneath the dark shadows of the pool.

Just then, a feeding trout dimpled the surface of the pool leaving a big bubble which swirled in the slow current of the pool.

"Thurp," said the trout.

"Thurp? How strange that the trout talks while it eats," muttered Bun-Bun.

"I wonder what it means?"

"Thurp," said the trout again from the end of the mossy log.

This time it was a deep, growling thurp which sounded
like a tub drain sucking up the last of yesterday's bath.

From the sound it made Bun-Bun knew that the trout was a big one.

And he knew that it was hungry. Bun-Bun wanted to catch that trout.
He fumbled in his fly box, and pulled out a big fly called a Rat Face
McDougal. Bun-Bun tied the fly to his line with trembling paws,
and began to cast.

"Maybe this looks like a Thurp," Bun-Bun muttered.

Swish-swish, swish-swish, Bun-Bun's line sang over the pool, and settled softly on the water.

The Rat Face McDougal landed just up stream from the mossy log with a fern on top. It floated with the swirl of the dark water along the log, and over the spot where the trout had been feeding.

Bun-Bun's heart fluttered and bumped as he waited for the trout
to gobble up his fly.

The trout nudged Bun-Bun's fly, gave it a sniff, then disappeared. Thurpless and uneaten, the Rat Face McDougal drifted past the end of the mossy log into the quiet water of the pool.

"Not Thurp," said Bun-Bun to himself.

He wiped a drop of anxious sweat from his forehead. The trout had refused his favorite fly. What was the trout eating?

"Thurp, Thurp," the trout splashed.

Bun-Bun desperately searched through his box for a fly
which would fool the trout. But which fly was right?

Just then, a small-tawny-mayfly fluttered up from the surface of the water,
and landed on Bun-Bun's wrist.

"Thurp? Yes, you must be a thurp," Bun-Bun slyly whispered
to the silent insect.

Bun-Bun knew which fly to use at last. He reached into his box and plucked
out a fly called a Brown Drake. It was the exact image
of the mayfly on his wrist. Bun-Bun quivered as he tied the fly to his line.

Bun-Bun's line swished over the pool again.
The Brown Drake settled on the water and drifted by the log.

"Thurp, slurp," gurgled Bun-Bun.

"THURP!" said the trout, when it shattered the surface of the pool,
and gobbled up Bun-Bun's Brown Drake.

Bun-Bun lifted his rod and set the hook in the jaw of the biggest brook trout
he had ever seen. The trout thrashed on the surface for a moment,
then plunged into the shadows below the mossy log with a fern on top.

Bun-Bun felt the strong throbbing pull of the trout as it sulked in the depths of the pool. Suddenly, the scarlet side of the trout flashed as it darted from under the mossy log, and leaped into the air in one last attempt to break free.

After its great leap, the trout was tired. Bun-Bun slowly urged the trout into
the quiet water at the edge of the pool. With a quick dip of his net
Bun-Bun lifted the giant trout from the water.

Bun-Bun stumbled to the bank of the stream, and laid his trout on the
soft-moist-moss. He gently removed his fly from
the beautiful brook trout's jaw.

"Certainly you are too wonderful to eat," said Bun-Bun.

"Certainly," agreed the brookie in its own caught-trout way.

Bun-Bun was a little sad, but mostly he was happy
when he waded into the stream to release his trout.

"Back you go to the depths of the pool, great trout," Bun-Bun said as he let
the brook trout of his dreams slip gently back into the water.

The trout paused near the surface of the pool. Then, with a flip of its tail the great trout vanished into the dark eddy beneath the mossy log with a fern on top. Only a ripple remained on the water where the trout had been.
Bun-Bun watched the little waves of the ripple melt into the pool.

"Hmm," he said. "Big trout."

The sun was setting behind the ridge above the stream. Dark shadows began
to drift through the woods. Trouting was over for the day.
Bun-Bun folded his rod and started for home.

On the ridge, Bun-Bun paused to listen to the fading sound of the stream.

"Thurp," he shouted with a grin.

He listened as the sound bounced through the trees to the stream below.